RETURN OF THE DJINN

ADAPTED BY KATE HOWARD

Scholastic Children's Books,
Euston House,
24 Eversholt Street,
London NW1 1DB, UK

A division of Scholastic Ltd
London ~ New York ~ Toronto ~ Sydney ~ Auckland
Mexico City ~ New Delhi ~ Hong Kong

This book was first published in the US in 2016 by Scholastic Inc.
Published in the UK by Scholastic Ltd, 2016

ISBN 978-1-407162-61-4

Printed in Slovakia by TBB

2 4 6 8 10 9 7 5 3 1

Papers used by Scholastic Children's Books are made from woods
grown in sustainable forests.

www.scholastic.co.uk

SIX NEW CELEBRITIES

"Cut!" cried Dareth. He and the ninja were on the set of their new TV commercial. "That acting *knocked me out*. You ninja are the hottest thing in Ninjago City!"

Dareth was right. After destroying the Cursed Realm, the ninja had become more famous than ever.

In fact, Cole, Jay, Kai, Lloyd, Nya and Zane couldn't go anywhere without drawing crowds. Whenever they were out in New Ninjago City, they had to hide from their fans.

Most of the ninja preferred the privacy of the *Destiny's Bounty.* But Kai loved having fans follow him around.

Onboard the *Bounty*, Cole was focused on his training.

"When one is a ghost," Wu said. "One may have new abilities. Focus and discover them."

Cole closed his eyes. He floated up into the air – and then disappeared. A moment later, he appeared again. "Did you see me?" he yelled. "I disappeared! I mean, did you *not* see me?"

"Very good, Cole," Wu said. "That's it for today."

A NEW MISSION

A few minutes later, Misako and Wu called the ninja together.

"What is it?" Kai asked. "Have the shops sold out of Kai action figures?"

"No," said Wu. "When you ended the Cursed Realm, one ghost escaped. And you know him all too well . . . Clouse."

"Clouse, the evil sorcerer from Chen's island?" Cole gasped.

"Yes. Security footage shows him buying a train ticket to Stiix," said Wu. "Go there and stop whatever it is he is planning to do."

"But Dareth wanted us to visit the hospital for that Grant-a-Wish thing," said Kai.

Lloyd cut him off. "We take orders from Master Wu, not Dareth. Lil' Nelson only has a broken leg. If his wish is to be a 'Ninja for a Day,' that day can be tomorrow. Let's suit up!"

A few minutes later, the ninja were soaring toward Stiix on their dragons.

"We're flying over Ninjago City," Kai said. "Why don't we drop by to see Lil' Nelson?"

"We don't have time," Lloyd said.

"Technically, we do as long as we do not meet any problems," Zane said.

NINJA FOR A DAY

At the hospital, the ninja went straight to Lil' Nelson's room. "As a part of the Grant-a-Wish Foundation, you are a ninja for the day," Lloyd told him.

"Could you stay and sign the other kids' casts?" Lil' Nelson asked.

"Wish we could," Nya said, "but duty calls."

Cole pointed out the window. Screaming fans and TV crews were outside the hospital. "Uh-oh. Looks like we've got company!"

"I don't see us flying out of here with these birds in the sky," Cole said. He pointed to a crew of news helicopters.

Lloyd nodded. "Cole's right. No dragons. If we're going to escape, we can't be followed."

"So what do we do?" Cole asked.

Lil' Nelson whipped around in his wheelchair. "You say I'm a ninja for the day . . . let me get you out of here! Call me *the Purple Ninja!*"

"This is as far as I can take you," Lil' Nelson said. "Follow the stairs to the rooftop. From there, take back streets. I'll hold them off here."

"Lil' Nelson," said Lloyd. "I mean, Purple Ninja . . . thanks."

"Thank *you*," Lil' Nelson said. "You made my wish come true."

"Looks like we lost them," Cole said as the ninja scrambled up to the roof.

"But the nearest rooftop is still too far to jump," said Kai. "Airjitzu?"

Nya shook her head. "I just learned how to make a water dragon. I haven't earned my Airjitzu suit yet."

"If we don't leave now, we'll never get to Stiix in time to stop Clouse," said Zane.

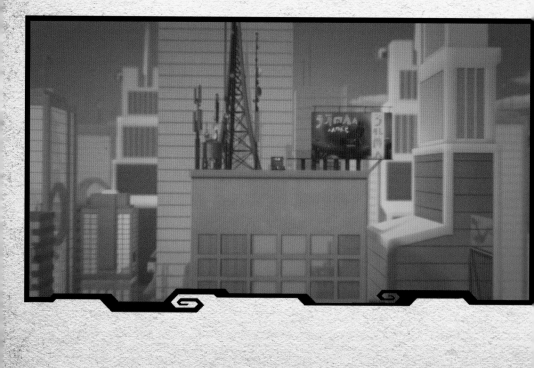

"We're a team," Jay said. "We stick together. Take my hand, Nya."

Nya shook her head. "Thanks, but I can stick up for myself."

"They're going to see us," said Lloyd. "Quick – take cover!"

"Just take his hand, Nya," yelled Cole. "Or else we will be spotted!"

He and the other ninja leaped up and hid behind a huge sign. But it was too late. The helicopters were back . . . and Nya was right out in the open.

"Let's hope Clouse missed his train," said Lloyd.

"Now what?" asked Cole.

One of the choppers spun around. Dareth was inside!

"This could be a big scoop," Dareth said. "Hop in!"

CLOUSE ON THE LOOSE

Meanwhile, in the village of Stiix, Clouse was hunting through heaps of trash. He had travelled a long way to find something very special.

"No . . ." muttered the ghostly sorcerer as he dug through the junk. "No . . . no . . ."

Suddenly, Clouse pulled a filthy teapot out of the rubble. "Yes! The Teapot of Tyrahn!"

Clouse rubbed the side of the teapot. "Work, darn you!" he screamed. He twisted the pot, trying to line up a series of markings.

Suddenly, the teapot began to glow. Clouse dropped it and backed away.

RETURN OF THE DJINN

Smoke flowed out of the pot. Then a shadowy figure appeared. It was Nadakhan the Djinn, one of the most famous pirates of all time. He had been trapped inside the teapot for years.

"I'm free?" Nadakhan asked. "Where am I? What year is it?"

"Nadakhan?" Clouse clapped. "I've freed a genie!"

"I prefer the term 'djinn'," Nadakhan growled.

"Who cares?" Clouse said. "I want my three wishes!"

Nadakhan nodded. "I must warn you. You cannot wish for love, death, and most certainly—"

Clouse cut him off. "More wishes. Yeah, yeah, I know the rules." He stepped forward. "I wish for my Book of Spells!"

"Your wish is yours to keep," said Nadakhan. A moment later, Clouse's spell book appeared.

"Ha!" Clouse said happily. "With my spells, who needs more wishes?" But when he touched the book, it burst into flames. "What's happening?"

Nadakhan chuckled. "You should have known the book was thrown into a fire. Perhaps you should wish for more than a pile of ash." He smirked. "Now for your second wish?"

Clouse thought. "I can't defeat the ninja as a ghost. I wish to be mortal again!"

"Your wish is yours to keep," Nadakhan murmured.

Clouse stared at his hands. They were becoming solid right before his eyes. "Yes! It's working. I can *feel* again."

But suddenly, he was overcome with pain. "Agh! My hands, my head . . . the pain!"

Nadakhan laughed. "Yes, you can feel. Becoming mortal is a painful process. I wish it would be over soon, but it won't. You could . . . wish it all away.

"Wish it all to go away and you will be free from your pain, free from your poor choices, free from existence," Nadakhan went on.

"I wish it all to go away!" Clouse screamed.

Nadakhan chuckled. "Your wish is yours to keep."

Gold dust poured out of Nadakhan's teapot. It covered Clouse and began to suck him inside the teapot!

"Be careful what you wish for!" Nadakhan said.

PRACTICALLY PRICELESS?

A few minutes later, the ninja had finally arrived in Stiix. They put on disguises to avoid being spotted. Then they began searching for Clouse.

After half an hour, the ninja regrouped. "He isn't here," Zane said.

"He could be long gone by now," said Cole.

Kai grinned. "But look what I found in the bin! A Kai action figure. No way anyone threw this out. It's practically priceless."

Lloyd pulled out his communicator. "No sign of Clouse," he told Misako.

"Keep looking," Misako told him. "Wu's at the Library of Domu trying to figure out what Clouse is looking for. If I hear anything, you'll be the first to know."

"Look!" Jay said, giggling as he poked around a junk heap. "Another Kai doll. There's dozens!"

Back in New Ninjago City, Nadakhan was having a hard time understanding a world that had changed since he'd been trapped in his teapot.

"You look lost. Can I be of assistance?" said a voice.

Nadakhan spun around. A computer with a display of Cyrus Borg's head was behind him.

"You are talking to Info-Vision," the voice explained. "Ask a question, and maybe I can answer it."

"Where is my crew, from *Misfortune's Keep*?" Nadakhan growled.

An image of a pirate ship appeared on screen. "The captain of *Misfortune's Keep*, Nadakhan the Djinn, was trapped in the Teapot of Tyrahn. His crew was marooned in separate realms."

"How do I get to these realms?" asked Nadakhan.

"You need the Realm Crystal. It is under the protection of the Masters of Spinjitzu," the computer replied.

"Tell me how to find them!" Nadakhan ordered.

WANTED: SIX NINJA

Back in Stiix, the ninja still hadn't found Clouse. So they stopped for lunch at a canteen.

A news report blared on TV. "They're calling it the crime wave of the century. Lloyd Garmadon was just caught on tape robbing the city bank. And at Mega Monster Amusement Park, Zane was on a rampage."

"Someone's pretending to be us!" Jay gasped.

"But who?" wondered Cole.

"The ninja are at large," a policeman said on the screen. "They are armed and dangerous. If you see them, call the police."

"Maybe now's a good time to leave?" Kai said.

"Hey," said one of the other customers, eyeing Zane. "Aren't you . . ."

"No!" Jay said quickly. "We're that other group with a Nindroid, a ghost, a girl and uh . . ."

Jay and the other ninja backed away as a mob of customers came after them.

"Six on six," Kai said. "At least it's even numbers."

Lloyd shook his head. "We're not going to fight. Right now it's us who look like the bad guys."

"How are we supposed to defend ourselves?" Jay asked. "Witty banter?"

"Run!" cried Nya. She and the other ninja raced along the boardwalk, then up and over the rooftops.

At the edge of a rooftop, the ninja had to use Airjitzu to get back on the ground. Jay held out his hand, offering Nya help. This time, she took it. "Thanks," she said.

The ninja ran again. But the crowd of villagers was close on their heels. "There's nowhere to hide!" Cole cried.

"There may be one place . . ." Kai said.

Kai used Spinjitzu to bore a hole through the floorboards. He and the others dropped under the boardwalk. Then they leaped across beams under the village.

"Mum," Lloyd said into his communicator. "We're in a bit of a jam!"

"I saw the news," Misako called back. "I am on the way. Looks like you've gone from fame to framed."

The ninja watched as the *Destiny's Bounty* raced over a bluff. Suddenly, a police officer yelled, "Take her down!" He fired a grappling gun and snared the *Bounty*!

The ninja's ship was trapped – and the ninja were stuck.

"We have a better chance of getting out of here if we split up," Lloyd said.

"But nothing good ever comes when we're split up," said Jay.

"We have no choice," Lloyd replied. He and the ninja fled in six different directions.

Back in the Library of Domu, Wu didn't know the ninja were in danger. But he *had* figured out what Clouse was searching for in Stiix.

Wu scanned the book in his hands, reading about the Teapot of Tyrahn. *"Be careful what you wish for.* Hmm."

Behind him, Nadakhan chuckled. "Did somebody say *wish*?"